Sassy Girl

*Who says plus size girls can't be sexy and play
the game too?*

A Novella By

Traci Glover Walker

Acknowledgements

I'm grateful, God, for so many things. I'm grateful for my friends. Even if I were to have only one good friend in my life right now, I would still be grateful. You showed your love for me through my friends in ways I sometimes overlook. They give me advice whether I need it or not, but in both cases, it shows they care for me. They listen to me complain, which I can do too much sometimes and they celebrate with me even when things aren't always going well for them. They help me to laugh at certain situations and even laugh at myself. That alone is reason to be thankful. Help me to be a good friend in return, God. I'm grateful to be part of a family that has helped make me the person I am today. I know they love me the best they can. Help me to be a good family member and to love them with all of my heart in return.

To my cousins Michelle Starling Clark, Tameka King, and Tonya Bennett McCray, thank you for your everlasting support. Shelia Gordon, words cannot express how grateful I am for you. Thank you for putting your life on hold and stepping up to take that role. You didn't have to do it, but you did. Charlette Footman, Marcy Bodiford, Kimberly Robinson, Amy a.k.a. Queen

Amy, and Stephen Phillips, thank you for your encouraging words. Charlette, you've been real with me from the first time we met. Thank you for not sugarcoating anything. Thank you for always keeping it "one hundred" with me, even if it hurts. Stephen, who has been a best friend to my husband and me, you've been there from the start. I know I'm hard on you, but please know we really appreciate you for everything. My spiritual sisters, Sherita Hart King and Letitia Hilliard, thank you for your prayers and the long conversations. I'm so grateful that God put the two of you in my life. Sherita, thanks for making me your baby girl's godmother. Teresa Edwards, my best friend, what can I say that you don't already know. We've known each other for years and have had our ups, downs, and misunderstandings, but we overcame them. We had periods where we stopped talking, yet you remained in my heart as if we were never apart. During that time, we became closer than ever and have both grown closer to God. Thank you for your trust, your realness, your encouraging words, your love as a friend and sister, and for being your true self. You never judged me nor did you try to change me. You accepted me for the person I am, and for that, I thank you.

My beloved husband, Julian, you have instilled so much in me. You encourage me to never stop believing in myself and to write from my heart. You've made me believe that it's okay to stay true to myself when I'm writing because people will relate to it. You never say much, but when you do, your words are profound. A man with few words is a wise man. Proverbs 17:27-28 (New Living Translation) says, "A truly wise person uses few words; a person with understanding is even-tempered. Even fools are thought wise when they keep silent; with their mouths shut, they seem intelligent." Thank you for your undying love and support. I love you with every bit of my soul.

Chapter 1

Just another day

Dear Diary,

Today was a beautiful day. I was able to sleep in and just lay around. I went out last night to the movies and dinner with my girls and I enjoyed myself.

Shawn and Val are my best friends. It was the first time we went out in a long time. After graduating from high school, we all went our separate ways. I left for college and earned a double major in design and business, Shawn went overseas to pursue a career in engineering, and Val attended the state college to study business and ended up starting a family. We stayed in contact by having long talks once a month to catch up on our lives.

After finishing college, I started an internship in our hometown. I was able to get an executive position with a great company and moved. Yet, I felt like something was missing in my life. I always wanted my own business. Since I had some money saved up, I stepped out on faith and started a design business named Luscious, selling everything from jewelry to lingerie. Still, that wasn't enough for me. In my heart, I felt I was missing something. I felt incomplete. I needed someone in my life who would love me, support me, and accept me for who I am.

Every relationship I was in might have started out good, but they sure ended badly. I guess that's why I bury myself in my work and don't make time to do anything. I don't even take time out for myself, but that needs to change. I really need to stop putting myself on hold and get back out there. To be honest, I'm scared out of my mind to start all over again, but I guess it won't hurt to go and have fun. On second thought, I'll keep doing what I'm doing and let it be. If I go looking for love, I'll find yet another snake like always, waiting to bite me at the first opportunity. I have to go for now, Diary. The phone is ringing.

"Hello?"

"Hey, girl! What's up?" Shawn's bubbly voice filtered through the earpiece.

"Hey, Shawn. Nothing much. What's going on with you, Sis?"

"Girl, same ole, same ole, that's it. I called to see if you have any plans for tonight."

"Not really, but I'm tired and just want to stay in and relax. Hold on, Shawn. The other line is beeping."

"Hey, girlie-girl!"

"Hey, Val. What's up?"

"Nothing much," Val stated. "What are you doing?"

"On the phone with Shawn."

"I'm going to hang up so we can do a three-way call, Okay?"

I clicked over and told Shawn, "That was Val on the other end. I'm about to call her so we can all talk."

"Okay," Shawn said.

The phone rang and when it connected, Val said, "Hey, girls!"

"Hey, Val!"

"So what are my girls talking about?" Val asked.

"I was asking Kay what her plans were for the night. I was thinking we should go out and have fun, but you know how Kay can be sometimes. She's so boring; she never wants to go out. Just work and stay home, acting like she's getting old," Shawn replied.

Val agreed, adding, "That is true, Kay. You don't have a life. Girl, you need to get out more and meet people. Maybe that way, you'll meet a nice man."

I tuned them out. To be honest, I was up working late most nights and was only getting about three to four hours of sleep a night. I wasn't thinking about meeting a man, going out, or anything else. I had a date with my bed, pillow, and blanket that I fully intended to keep.

I took a deep breath and blew it out. "Val, I'm exhausted. All I want to do is stay in and relax. And as far as meeting a good man, my mind is not on that right now."

What they didn't know was that I was definitely thinking about meeting a great guy. I wasn't about to tell them though because they would persistently aim to set me up on a bunch of ghastly "hook-ups" like they always tried to do.

Val replied, "All work and no play is not good, Kay. Loosen up a little."

"Yeah, Kay!" Shawn laughed out loud. "Let's have some fun, maybe a girls' night out tonight. We can go to the movies and dinner. What do you think?"

"Now that sounds good!" Val chimed in.

"What do you think, Kay?" Shawn asked.

"Come on, Shawn and Val. Really, I would like to just stay home and relax. Run me a hot bath and listen to some old school music."

They both kept after me until I finally gave in. Truth be told, I was kind of excited about the possibility of meeting someone.

"Okay, okay. What time should we meet up and where?" I asked.

"Let's meet at City Place around eight o'clock by Wet Willy's," Shawn stated, and Val eagerly agreed.

I still wanted to stay in, but I knew my girls wouldn't allow me. So, I agreed.

On that note, we got off the phone. It was six o'clock already, so I decided I should get up and get ready. I went upstairs and took a shower with my Victoria's Secret Coconut Passion. I thought to myself, Man this water feels good. Wish I could stay in all day just to relax.

Shutting off the water, I stepped out and applied the lotion and body mist. While doing that, I decided to wear my black, strapless dress with a couple of my own designs, a red butterfly belt with crystals on the wings and a pair of red and black heels personalized with my initials in crystals. I pulled my hair into a ponytail to show off the new black feather and beaded earrings I made. Once I took out my red purse to complete my ensemble, I was ready to go. Before leaving, I stopped and looked in the mirror. After a quick glance, I admonished myself. Now, girl, you looking like you going out on a date. I should just change into some jeans, a shirt, and tennis shoes and be done with it. However, I knew good and well if I changed, I'd throw on my comfy pajamas and call it a night.

Pursing my lips, I murmured, "Nah, I'll stay like this."

I got there around 7:10 p.m., only to discover Val and Shawn were already there. It was still too early for the movies, so we went inside Wet Willy's and ordered some drinks. I ordered a Shirley Temple, Shawn ordered rum and Coke, and Val chose a root beer. We laughed, talked, and went down memory lane. Before we knew it, it was time for us to leave. My watch indicated it was 7:40 p.m. We arrived at the theater and unanimously decided to see Twilight, which was good.

Afterwards, we went to Outback Steakhouse. I ordered a strawberry passion martini, the chicken artichoke flatbread, and for dessert, the gingerbread cookie martini. Shawn ordered the Outback special and ribs, with a Captain's Mai Tai, and Val ordered fresh fruit cocktail and the herb-roasted prime rib with lobster. For dessert, they shared the Oreo Cookies and Cream waffles. I was too tipsy to drive, so Val drove me home since we live close to each other. Shawn followed us so she could take Val back to get her car. I can honestly say I enjoyed myself.

Chapter 2

Memories

Shawn

I've known Kay since we were kids, our mothers are best friends. We stayed down the street from each other and shared everything. For as long as I could remember, Kay was always a loner. She never really had a lot of friends from what I could see. She's too kind-hearted and always watching after other people. It's long past time for her to watch out for herself. I'm tired of her always feeling down and out. She works so hard for people to not notice her. All she does is work and go home. Don't get me wrong, I'm happy for my girl. She came a long way from where she was. She started her own company and purchased a house and a BMW M3 Coupe. I can honestly say I'm a little jealous of her though. Kay has this thing I admire. Even though she's so hard on herself, she maintains a positive outlook on life. That's something I wish I had. A lot of people don't have that. She can always put a smile on peoples' faces and encourage them, even though she's having bad times herself. She's a fun person to be around and a good friend, but I can't stand the way she allows people to run over her, even myself. Although she allows that, don't get her wrong; she will put you in your spot and tell you what she thinks.

I had a great time with them tonight. I wish we could do it more often, but I have my own problems I need to deal with. I wanted to talk to them about what those problems are, but tonight, it was all about Kay. I wanted her to have fun and take her mind off the things she's been going through. See, Kay has been overweight since we were kids, but she never had problems getting a man. Kay is 5'9", plus-sized, caramel complexion, bowlegged, and has brown eyes with medium-length beautiful locs. She's not like some oversized women with their stomach hanging out and lapping over their clothes, acting like they don't know they have a big stomach and trying to wear clothes that don't fit them. Kay always dresses nice and looks good for her size. She can dress to kill and walks with her head held high despite the fact that she knows people are always looking at her because of her size.

One day, I was checking out this dude, Mikeo when we went to the Improv in City Place. He was 6'1", had a light brown complexion, and wore his hair in cornrows braided to the back. Mikeo had on a graphite heather Nautica quarter-zip mock neck shirt, a pair of Nautica, dark rinse jeans, with a khaki, Nautica twill overlay jacket, a leather belt and some Stacy Adams Pedigree boots. He was looking fine and smelling good. We were seated at a table in a back corner, chilling out and talking when along came Kay and Val messing up the mood. He was all into me until they showed up. Then, out of the blue, Kay had his full attention. I wasn't surprised because she is beautiful and carries herself with the style and grace of a runway model. I was pissed though. So much so, I wasn't even going to introduce them. Yes, I have a very jealous streak, and I make no excuses for it. Kay has everything I want in life. I wasn't about to hand over the man I liked too. He was mine and we worked well together. I fully intended to keep it that way. I was checking him out every time I went to either the Improv or B.B. King's Restaurant and Blues Club. However, this particular night he was all into Kay, even when we went to the restaurant he couldn't keep his eyes off her.

I started asking myself, What does she have that I don't? I had the body every man wanted, nice clear skin, and a booty you could bounce a dime off of. I work hard for my body. Who does she think she is? I know we're girls, but come on, I look better than her. I know that sounds awful to say because that's my girl, but he will be mine. I've always been jealous of Kay. I think I'll have to teach her a lesson about not crossing my line. Girls or not...

Val

What can I say, my girl was tipsy and she had fun. That was the goal for tonight, right? It was nice for us to get a chance to get her out to enjoy herself. She's been working like crazy and staying home all the time just because she got hurt dealing with that no-good dude Mikeo we met at the Improv. Sure, he was good looking, but he wasn't all that. Kay was feeling him from the moment she saw him. She didn't think he was going to talk to her; she has a serious complex and thought every man that looked good wouldn't want to be bothered with her like that. But to her surprise, he stepped to her and started talking to her. Ever since then, they've been together.

I never did like him, I felt he was using her from the beginning to get what he wanted. There was something about him that didn't sit right with me. I tried to tell Kay about him, but you know how it is when you tell your home girl the deal about someone they're into, they don't listen. Mikeo was a ladies' man and a thug. For the life of me, I really didn't understand why she liked thugs.

Mikeo had this thing about him; he carried himself like a star. Dude was straight smooth with it, he told you what you wanted to hear, and that's what made you feel good. Hell, I even wanted to get with him just to have sex. I wanted to know what he was all about with his manhood. I wondered if he can work it like the other chicks said he could. Can he eat the clit right and tight? It would only be just sex between us because I need that fix. Of course, Kay doesn't need to know and I hate to go behind her back, but I tried to tell her that he was no good. I guess I'll have to be the one to prove it to her.

Kay deserves what she gets. When we were younger, she always acted like she was better than Shawn and me. She went off to college and came back acting worse than she was before she left. Don't get me wrong, I love my girl, but I have to get me first. Kay always ends up back on top when she falls, so hell, why can't I be happy, even if it's for sex? It will hurt Kay, but shoot it's time I come first. After all, you know what they say... 'there's a dog in every man and a whore in every woman'.

Mikeo

Who is this girl? Fine, sexy, and bowlegged. Damn, she's nice and thick. I like my women with some meat on their bones.

When she walked in the club with that other chick, it was like she was the only woman in there. Everything stopped for a second, and I had to catch my breath. I started daydreaming on the spot about the things I would have her doing to me and with me. I can't stop thinking about her. She walks with class and confidence. That's such a turn on. Her curly locs were pulled back to show her beautiful face. She was shaped nicely to be a plus-size woman, with a thick booty you can hold onto while you're . . . I can imagine sticking my long shaft into her mouth and her sucking the tip slowly, waiting for the cream to escape. Grasping it with her freshly manicured hand, she carefully licks my head, sucking harder and harder until I explode. Then I slowly kiss her neck and pull her close to me. I've been thinking about her ever since we met at the club, and best believe she'll be one of my victims. I need a new toy to play with and I just found it. Okay, I need to snap out of this and work my magic on this beautiful lady. I have to know who she is and what she's about.

Yes, it looks like this game will be very interesting.

Chapter 3

Feelings

Kay

Good evening, Diary! Two weeks ago, Shawn invited Val and me to the club she goes to all the time. I was feeling down and lonely, so I decided to go. Besides, I always wanted to check the place out. I heard some great things about it, so I went. Like always, I had a hard time figuring out what to wear. I can't go half-stepping. I have to dress sharp because all my friends look better than me. Being the only fat girl in the group, I have to look at least half as good as them. Sometimes, I feel like they only invite me places so they can feel good about themselves. You know, in every group of friends you have that one ugly or fat friend that holds the purses, keeps the seat warm, or stands on the sidelines. I refuse to be that friend, it won't be me doing that.

Looking in my two-door mirrored closet, I searched through my clothes to figure out what I could wear. Oh yeah, here it is! I felt like putting on one of my Baby Phat outfits. So, I took out the red, one shoulder, printed shirt, the Baby Phat Whitney flare jeans, and my black Baby Phat

Chance platform pumps. I decided to accessorize with a three-level rhinestone pearl bracelet, red crystal cube necklace, and red cube earrings that matched. I had to show off my own designs as well.

I needed to burn off some stress and have fun. Those chicks won't have me holding their purses all night. By the time Val and I arrived at the club, it was packed wall-to-wall. Man, you could barely get through to walk. Val and I were shoulder to shoulder walking to the back. Suddenly, I saw this good-looking man sitting in the back of the club with Shawn. I figured him to be the type that would never look at me. He looked like a man who only went for a thin woman and would never give a plus-sized woman a chance.

I put on my best smile, held my head up, and walked through the crowd like I was the only woman up in there. I refused to let my low self-esteem beat me down. It's funny, Diary, how my friends believe I think so highly of myself, but it's just a mask I put on. I wear it to show them I can look good just like them. I have to work extra hard due to my weight issues though. I know how they feel about me deep down. I know they want what I have. Diary, I love my girls, but they're always thinking of themselves. Why can't I have some true friends? I've known these girls since we were small. I know friends grow up and sometimes grow apart, but the things they do and say sometimes makes me question our friendship.

Talk to you later, Diary. I'm going to soak in some warm bath water.

The Improv and B.B. King's Restaurant and Blues Club

Walking through the crowd, I saw Shawn waving for me and Val to come over to where she was. I tapped Val's shoulder and pointed in the direction of Shawn to let her know Shawn was waving at us.

Val turned around and asked, "Kay, who's that guy with Shawn?"

"What guy? I don't see a guy." I decided to play with her and act like she didn't see him.

"Kay, look. He's on the right hand side of her, that handsome dark chocolate man."

"The only man I see on the right hand side is that light brown man."

"No, the other one."

"You mean the one that's looking this way, Val?"

"YES! That's the one I'm talking about. Girl, you need your glasses," Val said, laughing. "How could you not notice him right off the bat?"

"It's the lighting in here."

Val looked at me incredulously and laughed again. "Yeah right, Kay. With or without your glasses, he's still fine."

"Val! You're always talking about this man or that man is fine. Not once have I ever heard you saying a man is ugly or not your type."

"Kay! Are you looking down on me?"

"No, Val. I'm just saying every time I turn around, you're saying some man looks good."

"Well, Kay, so that's how you feel? At least I can get a man to look at me."

"Hold up, Val! I know you didn't just go there with me. Umph! It's all good, girl. Say what you want."

Shawn walked over to where Val and Kay were standing.

"Why are you two arguing?" Shawn asked.

Val immediately went into defensive mode. With a manicured finger, she pointed at me accusingly and said, "Kay making her smart remarks like she always does."

"Val just can't take the truth."

Shawn shook her head and proceeded to scold the two. "You two need to stop. We're here to have fun and blow the town up. Come on, I have someone I would like you to meet."

Walking over to the table, Val looked happier than she ever did. Don't know if it was because of her new haircut or what, but she was acting all cheerful. My mind went blank, and I zoned out.

"Kay... Kay... hello! Earth to Kay."

"Oh, sorry!"

"Where were you just now?" Shawn asked. "I was calling you for like a minute or so."

"Sorry, I was in deep thought."

"Val and Kay, I would like you to meet Mikeo."

Everyone introduced themselves, and Shawn continued to speak. "Mikeo is a co-worker of mine. He works in the Human Resource Department with me. He's my boss, I asked him to join us tonight, so let's have some fun."

Everyone made small talk for a minute, and then it happened again.

Val and Shawn went to dance, and like always, I ended up being the purse keeper. Mikeo left briefly, but came back.

"Hey, beautiful lady, why are you sitting here alone? May I join you?"

"Sure."

"May I say, you look amazing tonight?"

He's just talking. I know he just wants to get into my pants tonight. I won't be rude and I'll still thank him though.

"Thank you for the compliment."

"What's wrong? It seems like my compliment made you uncomfortable. Are you okay?"

"I'm fine, and it didn't. So, Mikeo, what brought you out here with us tonight?"

"Well, since I come here all the time, I should be asking you that question. This is my first time seeing you here."

"Yeah, I don't get out that much. I'm a serious workaholic."

"I love a woman that has a great work ethic, but you have to get out and have some fun."

"Yeah, I hear that all the time."

"So, Kay, what do you do for a living?"

"I have my own business called Luscious. I design everything from jewelry to lingerie."

"So you're doing well for yourself? That's great."

"I get by." As I looked up, she saw Shawn and Val looking our way. I bet they're wondering what we're talking about, she thought smugly.

When I looked up again, Shawn was approaching the table. She was smiling, but I knew behind that smile, she was smoking hot.

"So what's going on over here? You two sure seem to be getting close."

"Excuse me. I have to go to the ladies' room." I said rising from my seat and walking away, determined not to let Shawn get under my skin.

"Wow, did I interrupt the two of you?"

She knows damn well she interrupted us, Mikeo thought to himself, but instead replied, "No, Shawn, you didn't interrupt anything. We were just talking."

"So why did she leave so fast?"

"I don't know," Mikeo stated.

The only reason Shawn came back to the table was to make sure Kay didn't hook up with Mikeo. Kay didn't understand Shawn sometimes. Why couldn't she just be real?

Shawn started talking to Mikeo and making obvious passes at him, but he only had eyes for Kay. Val decided to come back to the table. She couldn't stand that Shawn was talking to Mikeo and fawning over him like she was.

"Climax" by Usher came on and Shawn instantly started swaying to the music. "Ooooh, that's my song," Shawn said. "Mikeo, would you dance with me?"

He stood up and extended his hand. "Sure."

Shawn grabbed it eagerly and practically dragged him to the dance floor.

Val cut her eyes at Shawn, but Shawn laughed and kept going. Kay came out of the ladies' room just in time to see Shawn and Mikeo dancing like they were lovebirds. Val was so jealous that she cut between Shawn and Mikeo. She couldn't believe what she was seeing. Her best friends were acting crazy over a man who probably didn't want anything to do with either of them.

Mikeo stepped back and told them that he was leaving. He walked back to the table where Kay was sitting, while Shawn and Val stood there looking stupid with their mouths agape. They were in disbelief that Mikeo left them standing there looking like two fools.

"I'm ready to leave now," I announced.

"Do you want me to take you home?" Mikeo eagerly asked.

"Sure," was my reply, then I softly murmured, "Let's see how my girls react to this."

I walked over to the girls to tell them I was leaving and Mikeo was taking me home. I told them I wasn't feeling good, but the truth was I couldn't believe my friends were about to fight over a man. Val and Shawn looked at Kay incredulously when she told them Mikeo was taking her home.

Shawn replied back, "Did he ask to take you home or did you ask him?"

"He asked Kay."

"Girl, he was just being nice," Val stated. "Nothing else."

I looked at them with their half-smiles on her face. Once again, they made their feelings clear; a fat woman like me couldn't be appealing to a man.

On the way to my house, Mikeo and I had a nice conversation. During the ride, I thought about how intelligent and easy to talk to he was. A person I could definitely talk to and be friends with. The conversation was flowing so freely. I didn't notice when we pulled in front of my house.

"Thanks, Mikeo, for bringing me home and for the nice talk."

"No problem. Anytime. Listen, Kay, may I have your number?"

I was speechless for a second and then thought, What the heck? Why not? What harm could it do? "Sure, Mikeo."

He handed me his cell to input the number. He kissed me on the hand when I gave him the phone back. Kay smiled widely and unlocked the door.

"Good night, Kay."

"Good night, Mikeo." I turned around and saw him standing by his car waiting for me to go in the house. "Thanks again for bringing me home."

"It was my pleasure."

Once inside, I peeked out the window to see that he was back in his car with a smile on his face.

As I locked the door, I thought, why did I give him my number? What did I just do? What have I gotten myself into? Believe it or not, I didn't know what happened, but the rush I was feeling sure felt good.

I still couldn't believe how the girls acted. Then again, it was nothing new; they always acted like that. I was always the third wheel when it came to them. I always accepted that, but after that night, I made up my mind that I was going to concern myself with my wants and needs first. From that point on, I didn't care what they had to say. It's my life, and I'm going to live it on my terms. No one has the right to tell me what I can or can't do. I knew Val and Shawn were going to have plenty of things to say about their night out, and if they didn't say it, their actions would surely say a mouthful for them.

It's funny how friendships grow apart from jealousy. I admit, I have a lot of insecurities, but one thing's for sure I have always wished my girls the best. However, when it comes to me, I felt like they didn't feel the same way. I know there will come a time when will will have to talk about it and put everything on the table. The anxiety I'm experiencing from trying to be perfect like them needs to stop. God made everyone different for a reason. He didn't mean for people to look or act the same. So why do they try? Should I fight for the friendship even though I know Val and Shawn are as two-faced as could be? Or should I conduct myself like them? I really have to give it some more thought.

Chapter 4

Getting to Know You

Just as I started up the stairs to take a bath, my phone rang.

"Hello?"

"Hi, sweet lady. Are you asleep?"

"No. Who is this?"

"Mikeo. I had to see if this was your real number. Plus, I wanted to see if you were okay. I was thinking of you. I had a great time talking with you and wanted to ask if you would go out with me on Thursday?"

I couldn't help but grin like I hit the lottery. "Yes, this is my real number, and I'm okay. As far as going on a date with you, I don't know about that. I don't want your girlfriend or wife to come after me."

"I don't have a wife, and what girlfriend? I have friends, yes, but that's it."

"Listen, Mikeo, I don't want any problems."

"What problems, Kay? All I'm asking is for us to just go out, talk, have a little fun and get to know each other, that's it."

"Okay, Mikeo, tell me about yourself."

"What do you want to know?"

"Everything."

Mikeo grew totally quiet for a second. This girl is no joke, he started thinking to himself.

He took a deep breath before answering. "My wife and I went through so much together."

"Hold up," she said, shocked. "What do you mean your wife?"

"Yes, wife, but we aren't married anymore. So, I guess I should have said my ex-wife. Can I finish, please?"

"Yes, Mikeo. I apologize. Go on."

"We got married young. We thought by being married, things were going to get easy, but it only got worse. I didn't want to give up, but at the same time, my heart was being broken. I found out she was having an affair with her boss, and I just wasn't going to have it. So, I divorced her. After all this time, I'm still trying to get over it, but I have to move on."

"Sorry to hear that."

Inside, I wondered if he was telling me the truth or just telling me what he thought I might want to hear.

"So, Kay, enough about me. What about you?"

"Well, I'm not with anybody at this time. I'm too busy to be with anyone right now. The last time I was in a relationship was like a year ago. He wasn't ready for a serious relationship, and I wasn't about to just sit there and play house. Hey, Mikeo, it's getting late, and I have to go," I said, abruptly ending the conversation. "I'm very tired, and I have to get up early."

"Alright then, talk to you later. I hope you have a good night."

"Okay, goodnight."

"Oh, Kay, wait. Before you go, you didn't answer my question."

"What question?" I asked, smiling.

"Going out on Thursday with me?"

"Hmmm...I need to think about it. Okay, why not?"

After we ended our call, I hung up, headed to the bathroom and ran some warm water to soak in. I sat on the edge of the bathtub, pouring the Warm Vanilla Sugar bubble bath from Bath and Body Works. Lighting a Beach Cabana candle, I inhaled its pleasant aroma, it reminded me of a day at the beach. I cut the lights off, lowered myself into the water, and started daydreaming. Time flew right by, and when I realized the time, I jumped out the tub and put on a red, lace teddy. I smiled at my reflection in the mirror and thought, Not having a man doesn't mean I can't still dress sexy for myself.

I woke up to the sound of the alarm clock and thoughts running through my mind.

It's morning already! Ugh, I hate Mondays. Being on the phone with Mikeo late last night and going out didn't help. That reminds me, I have to call the girls to see what's up with them. They were something else last night. I never knew them to act that way before. I have a nine o'clock conference call and a ten o'clock appointment. What should I wear? All I can do is think about Mikeo and wonder if he was telling me the truth or not. Should I ask Shawn about him or just try to find out things for myself?

Time was getting away from her so she quickly pushed those thoughts out of her head and got dressed. She had already laid out a Ruby Rox one-shoulder, embellished, belted dress to wear with her Marc Fisher tranquil, black. Snake, platform sandals. From her very own line of jewelry, Kay chose a black crystal, chandelier necklace, black rhinestone, beaded earrings, black seashell, floral silver cuff, and a flower hollowed out, black ring. She twisted her locs up the night before so they would be curly; she shook them loose so she could wear them down. Then she put on coconut lip gloss, a little eyeliner, and was out the door.

Before she knew it, two o'clock hit, and Kay realized she hadn't eaten all day. *What can I get that's quick? As she sat there and pondered*, the phone rang.

"Hello?"

"Hello, beautiful lady. How are you today?"

"Doing fine, Mikeo. How are you?"

"Great now that I have you on the phone. What are you doing?"

"Nothing, I was just thinking about getting something to eat."

"Meet me at The Breakers within the hour."

"Why? What are we going to do at The Breakers?"

"Just come."

"Okay, see you in an hour."

What on earth is Mikeo up to? The Breakers is one of the finest spots in Palm Beach, Florida. They have splendid service, a stunning rooftop, nine on-site restaurants, and ten on-site boutiques. I love that place. Some of my clients like to meet there for discrete business meetings, Kay thought.

When she arrived at The Breakers, Mikeo was already there to greet her with a big smile and a huge bouquet of her favorite flowers, light pink and purple tulips. She didn't know what got into her, but she leaned over, kissed gently kissed on the lips, and thanked him. For a split second, he looked shocked, then he smiled and kissed her on the cheek. Kay wasn't expecting him to do that, but she took it with a huge smile.

He looked her over from head to toe and whistled appreciatively. "You look magnificent today, Kay. You're blowing my mind."

"Thank you, Mikeo. You don't look too bad yourself."

She held the flowers up to her nose once again and inhaled their fragrant aroma.

"So I see you love the flowers?"

"Yes, these are my favorite flowers and colors. How did you know?"

"I didn't. I just saw them and knew you would like them."

"Well, thank you again."

Mikeo took her arm gently and to guided her down the sidewalk. "Kay, let's step in and have some lunch."

They decided to go to Top of the Point, just a few minutes from The Breakers. Top of the Point has breathtaking views of the Intracoastal Waterway of the Atlantic Ocean. Kay was feeling like a princess. The two talked, laughed, and had a good time.

Kay and Mikeo decided to take a walk on the beach. Further up was a beautiful Cabana that had sheer fabric that swayed lightly in the warm gentle breeze. There were dark, masculine, wooden tables inside with white cushions to match the curtains. As they sat and watched the sunset, Mikeo tried to serenade her. It wasn't happening for Kay, but she loved his heart. At least he tried.

It was getting late, so they started walking back to where they were parked. He kissed her hand good night and they said their goodbyes. Kay felt giddy and smiled as she drove home. As she stepped in the house, she received a text message from him.

Just seeing if you made it home. Let's go on our first date Thursday. Had a great day with you. Sweet dreams, and I'll talk to you later.

Her face completely lit up as she read his message. She texted him back, *Ditto.*

On the way to the kitchen, Kay saw the answering machine light blinking. All the messages were from Val and Shawn. She forgot to call them to see what was up with them from the other night. *I'll call them tomorrow for sure*, she thought.

At that moment, all she wanted to do was sip a soothing glass of her favorite red wine, and reminisce about her day with Mikeo.

She loved light and fruity wines, and the one she was enjoying tasted good.

Chapter 5

Something Wrong and Out of Place

Dear Diary,

Val and Shawn has changed a lot since I came back from college. Every time I'm around them, I feel like I'm the third wheel or something. I see how they act and talk to me with no respect when we're around men. It's like they don't think I can get one or either they don't want me to have one. They're always putting me down. That's why I've started distancing myself from them a little. But I'm trying to give them the benefit of the doubt.

Mikeo and I hit it off pretty good. At first, I wasn't sure what his intentions were, but now that I'm getting to know him more, he seems to be a loving and caring person. Still, I have to keep my wall up because I'm afraid of being hurt again. I want to give in and try again, but you know my heart has been broken before. Zylin was the love of my life in college. He told me he would never leave me and that we were going to get married. I was completely devastated when I found out it was nothing but a lie. I thought by giving him everything it would've made him stay, but it didn't. I thought by playing house with him that he would know I was a real woman and he'd stay, but he didn't! Cooking, cleaning, dressing classy, being successful, what am I supposed to do when a man doesn't want the good in you? I'm tired of all these tears. I need a real man, not these little boys. I need someone who is going to take these painful tears and replace them with joyful ones. I have flaws. Yes, I admit that, but who doesn't? This looks like yet another night I'm going to dream, wish, and think about the man who one day will come into my life and show me love. But where is he? Is he Mikeo?

Diary, I need to exhale...

Val

I can't believe Kay left with Mikeo. How could she? She's gotten beside herself now. She hasn't called me or Shawn since the night we all went out. Now that I think about it, I called her and she didn't call back. Something's going on and I'll find out. As for Shawn, I don't know who she thinks she is; I saw how she was trying to get up all on him, but I think not. I have to put these girls in check, best friends or not.

43

That reminds me, I need to call Shawn to see what's on that chick's mind. I dialed her number; there was no answer, so I left a voicemail. I need to know if she's interested in Mikeo and if so, I have to start making my move. I got his cell number when all of us were at the club; I slipped mine to him on a napkin when the girls weren't looking. We've been texting and talking a lot.

While sitting here trying to figure out what's going on with my girls, I decided to send him a text message.

Hey, Mikeo! What's going on? Do you want to hang out sometime this week?

Hey, Val. What do you have in mind?

I was thinking about going to Okeeheelee Park on Thursday.

Can't. I have plans on Thursday, lady.

What kind of plans do you have?

Just going out with a friend.

Well, let's do it on Saturday around noon then.

Sure. Goodnight.

Goodnight.

Hmm...He usually tells me what he's doing and who he's doing it with. Why is he being so secretive now? I definitely intend to find out.

Shawn

I can't believe Val was acting the way she was, like she owns Mikeo or something. She just doesn't know that I'm in the game to win. I wasn't even trying to really get at him, but since she was acting all crazy and Kay just up and left with him; I'm going to show them what's really up. I didn't even hear my phone ring, but when I picked it up, I saw a missed call from Val. I don't even want to talk to her right now. Kay is the person I really want to talk to, but she hasn't called. I know she works sunup to sundown, but a little birdie told me that she didn't come back to her office after the appointment she had today. That's not like her at all. Something is definitely up. I'll be sure to call her tomorrow to get the 411 on her tail. Meanwhile, I'm going to get the details on Mikeo so I can see what he's all about.

I really need to chat with Val and find out what her problem was though; giving off that attitude like Mikeo was her man. She should know by now that no man is truly yours until he puts a ring on your finger and even then you have to watch him. Every man is a dog in my eyes.

Mikeo

I had a perfect day with Kay. She's just what I imagined she would be, smart, funny, intelligent, and outgoing. She's a little shy, but I can break her out of that. She could be the one for me. I'll admit I was completely wrong about her when I first met her. She's very classy and I love that.

I have to make some serious plans for our first date on Thursday. I can't stop thinking about her. I feel bad not telling Val that I have a date with Kay. Val and I have been kicking it for a while, and when I need a release, she's the person I go to. It's nothing serious, just an occasional booty call.

Shawn was looking pretty nice that night too. Lately, I've just wanted to focus on Kay, but I don't know if I can be a one-woman man. After my divorce it seemed to me that I couldn't trust a woman. I haven't been serious with any of them, but I'm really feeling Kay. She's different from any woman I've ever gone out with. All I want to do is shower her with gifts and make her happy. I know me though, when the next woman comes along, I'll be chatting it up with her. Believe me, I want and need to stop. I want to know more about Kay. She's the first woman that's made me feel like my heart is beating again. I'd hate to hurt her; she's too sweet for me to play with. Speaking of which, I need to text her.

Hi, beautiful lady. I had to say goodnight to you again. I was thinking about you and our day together. Sweet dreams. I'll talk to you later today.

Hi, Mikeo, I had a great time, also. Thanks for today. Sweet dreams. Talk to you tomorrow.

Okay, sweet lady. Get some sleep.

Okay.

What am I doing? I never did anything like this, not even while dating my wife. Could she be the one to change me back to a good man? I know Val is thinking something's up because I didn't share my plans with her. She's probably going to question why I haven't been talking to her all that much lately. I can see she's trying to make her move. I told her straight up that I wasn't looking for anything serious. As for Shawn, I don't see her like that; she's probably going to be just for sex with me.

How can I break this thing up with her without breaking her heart? I know she has feelings for me, but I never acknowledged them because I didn't want anything from her but sex. She was my mean booty-call woman. She gave me what I wanted and more. If I asked her to have a threesome with her and Val, I know she would agree.

Although I'd love to have my cake and eat it too, something about Kay keeps making me think twice. I was like a shark after blood when I saw Kay. The way she talks and carries herself makes me want to know more about her. It's kind of strange to me because basically she's not my type. Don't get me wrong, I like my women with some meat on them, but she has a little too much.

It's incredible how Kay makes me feel without having sex with her; it's blowing my mind. I never knew a woman could make a man feel like this. I'm ashamed that I'm playing friends against each other. If you look at it from my point of view, I shouldn't be able to play them against each other if they are true friends. Kay has me open though, and she may be the one to turn me back around to the man I was in the past.

Chapter 6

Feeling Him

Kay

It's Tuesday, and I'm so ready for my date on Thursday. I have to go shopping to find me something sexy but classy to wear. I can't focus on my work at all; my mind isn't here at work. The buzzing of the intercom interrupted my thoughts.

"Yes, Cameron."

"You have a call from a Mister Mikeo."

"Thank you, Cameron. Please put him through."

"Hello, Mikeo. How are you?"

"Hi, beautiful lady!"

"This is surprising. What made you call me?"

"Well, I wanted to hear your beautiful voice."

"Oh, really? That's so flattering." I was grinning so hard that my jaws were almost hurting.

"Yes, really. How's your day going so far?"

"Ugh... slow. I'm thinking about leaving and going home to work. I have a quickly approaching deadline for a line of shoes that I have to present in two weeks."

"You will get it done. Don't stress too much. Are you going home?"

"Yes, I might as well. I think I'll be able to concentrate better if I do."

"Well, I'll talk to you later."

"Okay, Bye."

I pressed the call button on the intercom and spoke aloud. "Cameron, would you please come here?"

"Yes, Kay, you wanted to see me?" he said after entering my office.

"Yes, could you please cancel all of my appointments for today and move them to Friday? I'll be working from home for the remainder of the day."

"Okay, is something wrong? You haven't been yourself since this week started. I must say I like the fact that you've slowed down from working all night long."

"Yes, I'm fine. Just have a lot on my mind. I think I'll be able to work better at home."

"Does it have to do with Mister Mikeo?"

A big smile crept on my face when Cameron asked me that question.

"I think I got my answer from that huge grin on your face. Just be careful. I know how you love hard."

"Thanks, Cameron. I'll see you tomorrow."

"See you tomorrow, Kay. Have a good one."

Cameron is my best friend from college who has always had my back. He was there for me when Zylin broke up with me. That night, he sat up with me, losing sleep even though we had class in the morning. I ended up sleeping in his dorm room and he held me the whole nightlike he had feelings for me.

Confused about Mikeo, I decided I need to put it in God's hands with this quick prayer: God, I know you hear me and I ask you to help me out. I ask you to show me Mikeo's true intentions. Please don't let me fall for him if he is playing games with me and my heart. I'm falling for him; he's doing and saying all the right things. Lord, I open up my voice and I will worship you. My worship and my life is Yours. So, I ask you to show me. Speak, Lord. I need to hear your voice. I don't want to make another move until you speak.

Shawn

I guess I need to call Kay and Val since they haven't called me. I'll get in touch with them so we can have some drinks and I can see what's on their minds. We can meet at Blue Martini Lounge, an upscale bar that has a live band, great drinks and a VIP section.

"Hey, Val! What's going on with you?"

"Nothing, Shawn, where are you?"

"On Congress getting some gas, let's meet and have some drinks. Are you available?"

"I can make time."

"Okay! I'm going to call Kay to see if she can meet up with us. We really haven't talked since the club."

"Yes, it's been a minute. That sounds great."

"Great. Let's meet at Blue Martini Lounge off Rosemary Avenue. I'll see you in an hour."

I hung up and called Kay. Her cell went straight to voicemail, so I texted her.

What's up, girl? If you're not busy, meet Val and me at Blue Martini Lounge off Rosemary Avenue in an hour. We need to talk.

Within ten minutes, I got a text back saying she wouldn't be able to meet us because she was under a deadline and needed to finish some work. I texted back asking her to come out just for a little while.

This is just like Kay, always working. I think something is going on and she's hiding something. As far as Val is concerned, I have to keep my eyes on her. As soon as I stepped into Blue Martini Lounge, I got a message from Kay saying she's about 30 minutes away and she will see us soon.

Chapter 7

The Meeting

Val

I wonder what Shawn is up to. She didn't sound like herself. Does she know what's going with me and Mikeo? Come to think of it, she acted a little crazy at the club. How could I be so jealous? It's not like Mikeo and I are together. We just had a sexual encounter; I got caught up, and wanted more because I started having feelings for him. How did I allow myself to catch feelings? He was a smooth-talker and I was lonely. The truth of the matter is, I really want him because I think he's after Kay and I can't have Kay getting a man before me, especially a man that I like.

Kay

Shawn sounded like this get-together was important. I really don't feel like going; I really need to get this work done. We haven't talked since the club, and my mind just isn't focused on anything else at this time. Why did I tell her I was coming? If I keep putting this account off I'll lose it for sure. Then again, maybe it will be good for me to go and talk to them. It will get my mind off of Mikeo and this account, if only for a few minutes. Lord, I pray no mess is about to start. These girls have changed a lot, and I don't have the time or patience to deal with a bunch of foolishness right now.

Blue Martini Lounge

Shawn

So here I am sitting at the bar waiting on Val and Kay. I was thinking I should also call Mikeo just to spice things up. I would love to see their faces, all three of them. Something's fishy and I will get to the bottom of it. Kay has changed since she met him and Val acts like she has something to hide when it comes to Mikeo.

When Val walked in the door, I waved to get her attention. "Girl, what's going on? Why did you want to get drinks?" Val asked.

"I felt we needed to talk. I feel something is going on with you and Kay."

"Nothing's going on, at least not on my end." "Where is Kay anyway?" Val asked.

"She should be on her way soon. At first, she was saying she wasn't able to come because she

56

had a deadline, but I was able to get her to change her mind."

"Should we go ahead and order our drinks?" Val asked.

"No. Let's wait a little longer. I'm going to call Kay to see where she s."

Just as I pulled out my cell to call Kay, she strutted up to the table and sat down.

"What's going on, girlies?" Kay glanced at us as if trying to gauge our moods.

"Nothing much," Val and I replied in unison.

I stood up, smoothed my dress, and said, "Val and Kay, let's go sit outside to the patio bar."

We grabbed our purses and walked through the entrance where the patio was. Once there, we picked a corner table and sat down. Our waitress walked over to the table with some menus, silverware, and three glasses of water.

"Hello, ladies. My name is Skylar and I will be your waitress for tonight. Here's a menu. I'll be back in a few to take your order."

While Skylar was introducing herself, I was trying to figure out what to say. *How can I start off with the girls? Are they really going to tell me what's going on with them?*

"So, Kay, how's everything? I know you were telling me that you have a deadline, but I'm glad you came out. You need a break. Besides, we haven't seen each other in a while and we need to catch up."

"Yes, my deadline is coming quickly. I really need to be working on my presentation now, but you sounded like you needed to talk. So I figured I'd come see what was going on and why you made it sound so important."

"Kay, I don't know any other way to ask, so I'll just come straight out and say it. Have you been talking to Mikeo or have you seen him since the club?"

"No, I haven't."

I saw Kay purse her lips and get lost in the abyss of her thoughts. I bet she was wondering why I was asking her all the questions, or if Mikeo told me something?

"I've been too busy to talk or see anybody really. We talked after the club, and that's about it. He asked for my number, but you know how I am. Why?"

I looked at Kay intently and nodded my head. This ought to be interesting. "I see. You two looked very close at the club and I was thinking you two hit it off. Sure seemed like he was into you."

"No, Shawn, I don't think so at all."

"I think you two did hit it off. Kay, you're sitting here looking like you're hiding something that you don't want us to know." Val chided.

"Speaking of which," I turned to Val and pointed. "You've been sitting here acting like you have something on your mind so say it."

Skylar approached our table and interrupted the conversation. "Excuse me, ladies, are you ready to order?"

We all murmured in agreement as Skylar pulled out her pen and pad.

Starting with Val first, she said, "Okay, go ahead with your order."

Val folded her menu and asked, "May I have the Strawberry Bliss and the Lobster Salad?"

"Great choice. You will enjoy the Bliss. It has Grey Goose Le Citron, strawberry purée, sour mix, and cranberry juice."

Making eye contact with Kay, Skylar stood there, pen poised over the pad, waiting for her order.

Kay said, "Yes, I will have the Blue Crab Cakes and your Cake Pop."

"Oh, yes. You will love that. It's one of our new drinks. It's made with Three Olives Vanilla Vodka, champagne, a splash of cranberry, and garnished with a chocolate–sugared rim."

Turning to me, Skylar said, "And you?"

"Yes, I would like the Pretty in Peach and Shrimp and Crab Dip."

"You also made a nice choice. The Pretty in Peach has the nice taste of Bacardi Peach Red, Peach Schnapps, orange juice, and sour mix. Ladies, I will put your orders in and bring your drinks back."

"We need to get back to the subject at hand," Val said as soon as Skylar was out of earshot.

Kay immediately changed the subject. "Girls, I love this place. It's lovely outside tonight, with the wind blowing so gently. Isn't the band playing some nice music?"

"Yeah, yeah, don't change the subject, Kay!" I yelled.

"What's wrong with you, Shawn? Why are you yelling?"

Just then, Val piped in. She leaned forward in her seat and said, "Let's stop the nonsense Kay..."

Before Val could finish her statement, Kay cut her off. "Val, not you too!"

Kay was absolutely fed up with the nonsense and it was written all over her face. She sipped her water and sat the glass down. "If I had known you two would be all on me like this, I would have stayed home like my mind told me to. Where are all these questions coming from? I want them to stop now! I'm about to leave before I get angry and say something I'll regret later. I thought we were here to talk and get some laughs in. I've told you that I'm not hiding anything. What else do you want?"

Just then, Skylar and another waitress approached the table with two trays. "Here's your order, ladies, enjoy."

Simultaneously, we said, "Thank you."

Once the food and drinks were served, Val looked at Kay with a devious smile and said, "Spill it, Kay. Something is going on, I know it."

Blowing out an exasperated breath, Kay rolled her eyes upward. She sighed and started to explain. "Okay, fine. Mikeo and I have been talking regularly and I'm starting too really like him. He took me to Top of the Point for lunch the other day. We talked, ate, and relaxed. I had a great time with him."

"Is that all?" I asked.

"Yes, that's it. Now just let it go!"

"Hmmm... I don't believe you," Val responded. "I think more than that happened."

"Me, too," I said.

"Well, you can keep thinking whatever you like. I'm leaving! I have to finish my work and I'm a little offended at what you two are insinuating. I told you what happened and that's what it was."

Rummaging in her purse, Kay pulled out her wallet and snatched out a few bills. "Here's my money for my order. Bye!"

Kay got up and slammed her money down on the table. She walked off in a hurry and left the lounge, leaving us sitting there with our mouths wide open.

I was the first one to gain my composure. Chewing my bite of food thoughtfully, I reflected. There's definitely something about her that's changed. Suddenly, she has this newfound courage to stand up to us. She's not the quiet laidback person she once. We could snap our fingers and she'd do whatever we asked her to do. She needs to get back in her place.

"Shawn! What's wrong with you? You were sitting there spaced out. I bet you didn't hear a word I just said." Val yelled out.

"I'm good. Did you see that, Kay got beyond herself. She just going to get up with an attitude and slam her money down like she's all that," I spat.

Val nodded her head in agreement. "We need to put her back in her place."

"I'm leaving now. I'll talk to you later." I stood to gather my things.

"Hold up, Shawn. What about you?"

"What about me?"

"Since you had all these questions for me and Kay, I'm wondering do you have anything to say."

"No! Talk to you later. I have to go."

Val sat there seething as Shawn walked away.

Chapter 8

Tired

Kay

Dear Diary,

I am so tired of Shawn and Val. They really crossed the line this time. I used to sit there and let them talk to me any way they liked, do what they said to do, but now I'm so fed up with them. I don't want to be their sidekick anymore. I will start standing up for myself. I was so used to standing in the background thinking I wasn't sexy and didn't look good. Who says plus-size girls can't be sexy? I am sexy, smart, and beautiful. How could they think I did something with Mikeo? They should know me better than that. I'm beginning to wonder if one of them has something going on with him. They set that meeting up just to get some information from me. I should've known something was up; they don't just meet up in the middle of the week for nothing.

I heard the phone ringing and wondered who was calling me late at night. It better not be them.

A big smile appeared on my face when I saw the name on the caller ID. It was Mikeo. I eagerly answered the phone, jumping for joy on the inside.

"Hi, gorgeous!"

"Hey, you."

"Were you busy?"

"No. I was just sitting here writing and thinking."

"Thinking about what?"

"Nothing much, just work and getting this presentation done."

Every time he speaks to me or is around me, I get butterflies. I haven't felt like this in such a long time. Kay thought.

"So, Ms. Lady, are you ready for our date tomorrow?"

"It's Thursday already?"

"Yes, it is and I'm looking forward to it."

"I am, also. What time should I be ready?"

"Great! I'll pick you up around six o'clock tomorrow evening. Be ready, my love. Goodnight and see you tomorrow."

"Goodnight, Mikeo. I'm going to finish the last of my writing before heading to bed. See you tomorrow."

He gives me chills every time I speak to him. I don't want things to go fast with him; I need to slow down my feelings for him. Am I feeling this way because I'm lonely? Is he just trying to get into my pants and telling me what I want to hear? Why does he want to be with an overweight woman anyway? Look at me. A man like that doesn't want to be with a person like me. Yes, I have my own business and have a house and car, but what else can I offer this man? Not a thing. I'll be surprised if he takes me to a public place with people around so they can stare at us and wonder why he's with me. Well, goodnight, Diary. I have to get up early. Hopefully, next time I write I'll have more answers than questions.

Mikeo

Something about this woman has me intrigued. I've never actually been out on a real date with a plus-sized woman before. Her mind just blows me away. She's not like other women I've been with. I have to really deal with Val and Shawn. I know Shawn likes me and since we've played around here and there, I know she's developed feelings for me. As for Val... well, we were just playmates. It was all about the sex from the get-go. If I really want to be serious with Kay, I have to put an end to messing around with both of them.

I think I'm falling in love with Kay. But before I say the words "I love you forever", I have to first ask myself if I'm ready. I think I'm ready for love, but I'm not sure about the forever part. Love and forever are a big deal and you just don't throw them around like that. I told myself that I would never let my heart feel for anybody ever again after that fiasco with my ex-wife. I guess God has other plans for me.

Never in a million years did I think I would fall for someone like Kay. She's not my usual type to be in a relationship with, women like her I generally just play around with. When I set my eyes on her the first time, I only wanted one thing and that was her body. I just wanted to hit it and quit it as they say. I wasn't trying to catch feelings, I was only trying to catch a sexual release. But when we went out and talked, her brilliant mind and sparkling personality caught me by surprise. No other woman has ever captured my attention like that, not even my ex-wife. When she talks, I can feel her soul and how caring and giving she is, how passionate she is about God. She's made me look at life in a whole new light.

Chapter 9

Thursday

Val

I need to talk to Mikeo to see what's going on with him and Kay. This can't be happening. How can he go out with someone like her? Kay is big, fat, and nasty. I don't know how he can pass up a body like mine. I work hard to keep my figure looking good, and Kay's body is nowhere near as in-shape as mine. She reminds you of a giant blob when you see her. I turn heads when I walk into a room and men give me anything I want. I'm the woman all men like to show off. I even have a key to his place. So, what's so great about Kay? What does she have that I don't? That heffa thinks she's just going to swoop in and take my man, but I've got news for her.

It's eight o'clock in the morning, he usually leaves for work around eleven. I'm going to his house to see what's up. If I call, he'll only blow me off like he did the other day. I know the perfect outfit to wear. He loves when I wear sexy lingerie under my clothes, but this time it won't be anything but lingerie under my coat.

Arriving at his place, I entered quietly and the only thing I had on my mind was knocking his boots so good that he won't want to be with anyone other than me again. I continued down the hallway and heard the sound of water running, so I proceeded to the bathroom. There he was soaped up good in the shower. He was so into bathing that he didn't hear me come in.

"Hey, baby."

"Val! What are you doing here?"

"I miss you, that's why I'm here. What! You don't want me here?"

"It's not like that. You just don't come into someone else's place without asking for their permission."

"Oh, you never said that before."

"Because I knew you were coming. Now it's different and I want my keys back."

"Okay, but first, let me help you relax."

"No, you have to get out now. And put some clothes on, will you?"

"Mikeo, what's up with you? You're acting like a different person."

"Nothing, Val. I just need to be somewhere before I go to work."

I wondered silently if he was meeting up with Kay. "Where do you have to go?"

"Why are you suddenly asking all of these questions?"

"Because you've changed, you're not acting like you want to be with me."

I started kissing and rubbing him in places I knew would turn him on. I hopped in the shower and I started doing things guaranteed to make him scream out my name over and over.

By the time he realizes what's happening to him, there's no way he can deny how he feels about me when we have sex, I thought to myself. Kay can't satisfy him like I can, she can't even come close to it.

"Val, you have to go. Give me my keys."

I shook my head to clear it and tried to process my thoughts. What just happened here? He's kicking me out after all that I just did?

"How can you kick me out and ask for your keys? Didn't we just have mind-blowing sex?"

"Sorry, Val, but what just happened shouldn't have happened. I can't have this type of relationship with you anymore."

"Why?"

"I've started dating someone and I really have feelings for her. I want this to work out for us."

"Who is she, Mikeo?"

I already knew who it was, I wanted him to say it in my face. I wanted him to have the nerve to pick that fat cow over me. Yes, I call her my friend, but only because she makes me look good when we go places and she pays for almost everything. We've known each other since school, but even back then, I felt the same way.

"It's Kay."

"Kay! I can't believe this! You're picking her over me? I think not. This is not over. You better tell her about us or I'll tell her. And I don't think you want me to do that. I'll hurt her precious feelings and yours as well. Understand?"

"Val, you don't have to be like this. Let's just end this and be done."

"No, we won't! I mean it. You either tell her or I will. You can't break this up just like that. You think you're going to use me and then throw me away? You've obviously lost your mind!"

"Val, you already knew it wasn't like that. You knew it was just sex between us. So why are you acting like this?"

"Acting like what? Did you ever think I had feelings? Did it ever occur to you that I was hoping whatever we had would turn into something other than sex?"

"I told you straight up when we started this that I wasn't looking for anything, Val. Besides, I don't want a trampy woman who gives it up so easily like you did."

Before I knew it, my hand connected with the side of his face in a resounding slap. "How dare you? I was good enough for you to get your rocks off and now you want to dump me just like that?"

Mikeo couldn't look me in the face as he stood there rubbing his. "It just happened, Val, I'm sorry. I never meant to hurt you. I wasn't looking for anything with her. My feelings for her happened unexpectedly and I want to give it a chance."

"Over my dead body you will! It won't happen!"

I dressed quickly, threw his keys at him, n stormed off and slammed the door. I hopped in my car and screeched out of the driveway while yelling, "I can't believe this! It won't last because I won't let it!"

All the thoughts bouncing back and forth in my head were completely jumbled. Silently, I started trying to sort everything out.

That fat cow will not have him, even if I can't have him. Who docs hc think he is? He really had the nerve to tell me that he likes Kay and wants it to work. And Kay? Some friend she is; she didn't even tell us that she was seeing him. She lied. I knew it was more to the story than what she said the other day. That's why she got mad and walked off. They're going on a date tonight, I see. He wasn't too worried about "working it out" with her when I was "working him out" a few minutes ago. It won't last long, he'll come back to me. Kay can't please him the way I can in the bed. What can she do with her fat self other than lay there like a beached whale?

Chapter 10

Clearing Things Up

Mikeo

What have I done? What just happened? It wasn't supposed to go down like that. I didn't intend for her to find out that way. I wanted to let her down gently. And why did I allow myself to have sex with her? I need to take the day off, get my head on straight, then call Shawn and talk to her. I need to clear the air with her also. God, give me strength, please forgive me for what I've done. I played with these women's feelings and now it's coming back to bite me. I played with their hearts because I was hurt and not concerned with anybody else's feelings but my own.

"Good morning, Swabs and Swabs Associates. This is Shawn speaking. How may I help you?"

"Hi, Shawn, it's Mikeo. Can you meet me when you get a break? I won't be coming in today, so please cancel all of my appointments."

"Sure, no problem. Where do you want me to meet you?"

"Meet me at Starbucks on Northlake Boulevard."

"Okay, I'll see you within the hour."

How am I going to tell her that I truly only want to be her friend and that's all? I don't want to hurt anyone else; I feel so bad. I didn't mean to fall for Kay and I didn't mean for everything to end up like this. I hope she understands because Val didn't. Now I have to stop Val from telling Kay before I'm able to tell her.

Shawn

As I walked toward Mikeo, all sorts of things were going through my mind. I wonder what's going on with him and why he needs to meet me. He's sitting there looking like he has a lot on his mind. This will be a great time to talk to him about Kay and where we stand. I know we didn't have anything serious going on, but we did fool around here and there. He should have known I wanted more. I need to know why he started messing around with Kay.

As I approached the table, he stood up to pull out my chair.

"Hi, Mikeo, so what's going on?"

"Hi, Shawn, I'll explain in a minute," he said, raising his hand to get the attention of the waitress. "Would you like something to drink or eat?"

"Yes, please. I'll take a Venti Vanilla Spice Latte."

The waitress brought my latte and I waited until she walked away before I started talking.

"Thanks, Mikeo. So what would you like to talk to me about or is it that you just wanted to spend some time with me?"

He took a deep breath and I sat up straight. I knew whatever he was about to say was serious and I wanted to be ready for whatever it was. Is this it? Is he about to tell me that he wants something more than the casual relationship we have now?

I tried to look calm and collected on the outside, but my insides were quivering like a bowl full of Jell-O.

"Shawn, I know we've played around in the past and I know how you feel about me. I asked you here because I need to clear the air with you. I feel we have a great business relationship and

I'm hoping after I say what I have to say that part won't change. I'm sorry, but I have to put an end to the arrangement we have now. I'd like us to be friends without the extra benefits. To be honest, I've been seeing Kay and I really dig her a lot. I think she may be my soul mate. She makes me feel things I've never felt before and I want to give us a chance to see where this is headed. Please forgive me if I've hurt you and you feel that I've led you on. That was never my intention and I apologize, Shawn."

"Mikeo, I knew what type of person you were when we started messing around. I even knew you were sleeping with Val. I didn't care though because I wanted you and my feelings for you enabled me to look past it. I can't stop how you feel about Kay, but my feelings are hurt because you didn't tell me earlier. Don't worry; this won't mess with our business relationship. I have even more respect for you now that you've told me instead of dragging this along and not being honest."

"Thank you so much for understanding, Shawn."

I can't believe this. He actually likes Kay. It won't last long, trust me. I'll make sure of it.

Smiling at him, I stood up, "We're both adults and I knew what I was getting myself into. I have to go. I have an errand to run before I return to the office. See you tomorrow, Mikeo."

Before I head back to work, I'll stop at the flower shop to send a little surprise to Ms. Kay Brown. She's about to get a rude awakening.

"Good afternoon, how may I help you?"

"Yes, I would like to send some daisies to someone."

"Daisies are so bright and full of warmth. They're sure to make someone you care about smile. I can send our signature Pitcher of Daisies, if you like."

"Yes, that would be perfect," I responded while smiling to myself.

"Okay, that will be thirty-nine dollars and ninety-six cents. Will it be cash, credit, or debit? Would you like to include a message to this special person?"

"Yes, thanks."

"Here you go. I picked out a lovely card and here's a pen. I'll make the daisy arrangement while you write."

I thanked the florist again and composed my message. Ms. Kay, everything you see is not perfect. There's a lie in every story. The truth will come out soon.

I handed the card and pen back to the florist and paid for the arrangement, including a nice tip.

"When would you like these to be delivered?"

"Can they be delivered today? Here's the address I want them sent to."

"Sure, they'll be delivered in about an hour. Here's your receipt and have a good day."

Let's see how she responds to that! Little Ms. Perfect thinks she can get everything, but I can't let her have him. Yes, I acted like everything was cool with Mr. Wannabe. He really doesn't want Kay; he just wants what she has. Kay is way too big and has nothing to offer a man like him. And for Val...what a waste! If he would have told me it was Val, then I would have had some competition. Val would give me a run for my money, but Kay? What kind of a match is she? That's like trying to put a square peg into a round hole. Her role is to be the sidekick she's always been and that's where she needs to stay. When I get done, she'll realize she's not a match for me. She's a low-class woman trying to roll with the big girls now. I knew something was up when she had the nerve to come at me like that the other day. She'll regret what she's doing. Going behind my back like that...who does she really think she is? She's not acting like a friend at all.

Chapter 11

The Delivery

Kay

The view from my office window is always beautiful. You can see the beach and when the sun goes down, it's a beautiful sunset. I have a date with Mikeo tonight and I'm really looking forward to it. I wonder what he has planned. I finally finished up my work, now I can let my hair down and have some fun. I decided to let my wall down so he can really get to know who I am. I can't believe I've grown to have feelings for him.

While sitting there daydreaming, I was startled by a sudden knock on the door.

"Come in, Cameron."

"Kay, you have a delivery. These gorgeous daisies just arrived for you," Cameron said as he walked in and placed the flowers on my desk. "Who bought these for you?" he asked.

"It has to be Mikeo. We have a date tonight."

"You mean the man you were telling me about?"

"Yes." I leaned over to sniff the fragrant aroma of the daisies and grinned from ear to ear.

"I need to meet him to make sure he's right for you. Open the card up so we can see what it says."

As I sat back down to open the card up, I couldn't believe what I was reading.

"What's wrong, Kay? Why do you have that look on your face?" Cameron snatched the card from my hands and read it out loud. "Ms. Kay, everything you see isn't perfect. There's a lie in every story. The truth will come out soon." Cameron stated, "You know this couldn't have come from him. He wouldn't tell on himself, especially in this manner. Who would send you something like this?"

My eyes squinted with a look of displeasure as I responded, "I have a pretty good idea who sent this, but they need to be real and step to me and not play games. I'm a grown woman and I don't have time to be childish. The other day Shawn and Val wanted to meet up to have drinks, but it turned out to be an interrogation. All they wanted to know was if I have something going on with Mikeo and whether or not we had sex. I told them no I hadn't slept with him, but we've been talking and seeing a lot of each other. They didn't believe me and kept pushing the issue. I got upset and left them there."

"Kay, something's not right. They're supposed to be your friends. If they're questioning you like that, you need to suspect their motives. One or both of them are either messing with him or like him. Watch your back around them. I know you've known them since you all were kids, but people change and it's not always for the good."

"Cameron, I've played this over and over in my head and I already know they're acting kind of shady. I'm sitting on the sideline waiting to see what their next move is going to be. I can tell you one thing; I won't be their sidekick anymore. Whatever game they want to play, three can play it. Like the card said, the truth will come out soon and whatever it is, I have a feeling it won't be good."

"Well, Kay, be careful," Cameron said in a concerned voice. "Hey, what time is your date?"

I jumped up and looked at my watch. "Man, it's already two o'clock? I have to go and get ready. He's picking me up at six. Thanks, Cameron. I'll talk to you later."

"Okay. Have fun!"

Chapter 12

The Pick Up

I need to get my hair done and there's not enough time to go across town to the salon. Maybe I can do something with it. I'm not going to give any more thoughts about that card. Whatever they intended to accomplish by sending it won't work because I won't be backing down this time. If it's a fight they want, then a fight is exactly what I'm going to give them, Kay thought.

After being stuck on I-95 for practically an hour, Kay breathed a sigh of relief as she pulled into her driveway and rushed inside the house.

Her cell beeped and a text appeared. Hey, lady. Wear something sexy but comfortable, see you at six.

Thank goodness he texted me, 'cause I really didn't know what to wear. Now I have some type of idea, she thought.

Kay went upstairs to her bedroom and started looking through her closet. She pulled clothes this way and that way while mumbling to herself. At that moment, she found exactly what she was looking for.

"Here we go!" she exclaimed. "I can wear this black, beaded tunic dress. I finally have somewhere to wear it. It's nude and fits me just right. I have the perfect shoes to match them, my lace peep toes."

Kay went over to her dresser and removed her jewelry box from one of the drawers. She pulled out her sterling silver, black crystal chandelier necklace and earring set.

The perfect set for a perfect night, Kay thought as she laid her outfit and accessories on the bed, and placed her shoes by the nightstand.

She continued to walk to the bathroom with a smile on her face and intent on taking a quick shower to freshen up.

"This feels good," Kay said aloud as she showered.

Afterwards, she dried off and applied lotion to her already silky-soft skin. Standing by the bed, she slipped into her dress, put on her jewelry, then headed back into the bathroom to do her hair up into a French twist. She placed a flower hair clip in her hair as a finishing touch.

Kay turned on the CD player to relax. She selected "It's Not Over" by Chaka Khan featuring LeCrae. She started dancing and singing to the song, belting out the part "Can't stop now... No running away... You got some living to do." Looking at the clock, Kay realized it was almost six o'clock. She ran to put her shoes on and dashed downstairs. Right before she reached the last step the doorbell rang.

Kay was surprised when she opened her door to see purple tulips placed on her doorstep and gardenia puddles spread down her walkway like carpet, with Mikeo standing there. Greeting Kay with a kiss on the hand, he reached out his hand and grabbed hers. Kay was too shocked to speak.

"Ms. Lady, you look fantastic!"

"Thank you, Mikeo. This is beautiful."

"You're welcome, Lady, I hope you don't mind me doing this. Don't worry about the mess. Someone will come by in the morning and clean it up. May I have your hand so we can go? I made reservations and I don't want us to be late."

Mikeo helped her step down from her doorstep and guided her to the car. Kay was still awestruck. He opened the door while she took hold of the bottom of her dress and gently stepped in.

Chapter 13

The Date

Kay and Mikeo arrived at the restaurant Cafe L'Europe just south of South County Road.

"I've always wanted to come here," Kay stated.

"Well, here you are," Mikeo replied, smiling at her.

They stepped in and the maître d' greeted them with a smile. Kay and Mikeo looked around admiring the ambience and enjoying the soft jazz music playing in the background.

"Table for two?" asked the maître d'.

"Yes, please, Mikeo replied."

"Right this way."

Mikeo helped Kay with her chair as the maître d' placed their menus in front of them.

"Would you like some champagne, sparkling wine or Merlot? Our specialty wine for tonight is an excellent Pinot Noir. I can have the wine steward bring some for you right away."

Mikeo smiled at Kay and asked her if she'd like something to drink.

"Yes," she responded. "I would love a glass of sparkling wine."

At that moment, the wine steward presented the wine list to Mikeo, who looked at it for a moment before making a choice.

"Bring us a bottle of Louis Perdrier Brut Rose and some fresh peach puree for Bellinies, please."

"Very good, sir."

Kay was unsure of the right words to say to Mikeo, so she busied herself with admiring the décor of the restaurant. She especially liked the blending of the brick beams with the golden yellow and brick-tone striped carpet. She also liked the soft blue and brick-colored chair cushions on the chairs and the accessories decorating the lighting on the brick posts.

"You've been awfully quiet. Is everything ok?"

"Yes! I'm overwhelmed and speechless, that's all. You didn't have to do this. I just don't know what to say, Kay answered."

Mikeo smiled warmly, "Just say whatever you feel."

Not sure where to begin or even what to say, Kay puffed her cheeks slightly. She decided to open her mouth and speak from her heart. "Please don't take this the wrong way, but I have something to ask you and I need to know. What do you want from me? What do you expect from me? I know I'm not the type of woman you normally go out with, so what are your intentions? And please be up front with me because I hate being lied to."

"Kay, I find myself thinking of you all the time; wondering what you're doing, if you're okay, have you eaten. I can't explain it. All I want to do is make you happy. The first time we met, I didn't plan on having feelings for you. I wasn't even looking for a committed relationship. All I wanted to do was have a good time with you. But when we sat and talked on the beach that day something happened. You weren't like any other woman I've ever been with. You had me thinking about my future and what I want in life. After my divorce, I didn't want to think of anything like that. Now I find myself thinking about having children and spending the rest of my life with the woman God sent to me. And I know it's you. I always told God that he would have to send me a woman that makes my heart beat strongly every time I see her and when I see you, my heart beats like that."

The wine steward poured a sample of the wine for Mikeo to taste. Mikeo nodded his approval and the wine steward poured for them both. Next, their waiter for the evening walked up and introduced himself.

"Good evening. Are you ready to order?"

"Yes, we are," Mikeo commented. "The lady will have the Roasted Crispy Long Island Half Ducking and I'll have your ten-ounce New York Prime Sirloin Steak. Thank you."

Mikeo turned his attention back to Kay as the waiter walked away with their order. Kay was blown away by his earlier response. She thought she was the only one feeling the same way, but she wasn't able to accept that just yet.

"Mikeo, how do I know this isn't a game you're playing?"

"Would a man go out of his way to do something like this if he was playing games?"

Kay looked deeply into Mikeo's eyes and stated, "I want someone who will love me for me, flaws and all. Someone who can't fall asleep without my voice being the last he hears at night and the first he hears in the morning. I want someone who will always hold my hand and never let go, no matter how many hands are out there waiting to be held. He has to be someone who means it when he says, 'I will never leave you.' When he looks into my eyes, he sees his forever. Do you understand what I'm saying, Mikeo? Because if not, let me be and we can go our separate ways."

Mikeo gently took Kay's hands in his and asked her to give him a chance. He promised that he would never try to hurt her and he would give his heart to her.

After they finished eating dinner, they went on stroll along the beach to talk, laugh, and enjoy each other. The air was cool with a slight breeze, so Mikeo took his jacket off and placed it around Kay's shoulders. The moonlight was shining so bright they could see their refection in the water. The waves coming slowly up on the shore hit their feet while they were walking. The whistling of the sea birds singing added the perfect touch.

When they arrived back at Kay's house, he opened the car door and walked her up the front steps of the porch. He took her keys and opened the door, kissed her on the cheek, placed one of the purple tulips in her hair, and bid her goodnight. He waited until she walked in and closed the door before he left to get in his car.

Chapter 14

Confused and Scared

Dear Diary,

Here I go again, caught up with a man who I really don't know. Does he truly like me or is he just playing mind games? He says he likes me and wants to have a family with me. But, I'm still all torn up about Zylin. I had a wonderful time with Mikeo; he did things for me no man ever did before. He made me feel so special tonight and I didn't want the night to end. He didn't try to come in for a nightcap or even try to kiss me on the lips. I'm so confused and scared.

Diary, I still love Zylin, but I already know I can't have him. I don't want to feel like this anymore, but I can't stop because he was the one I gave my heart to. He took me for granted thinking I'd always be there, and I was. He mistreated me and made me feel worthless because he knew I'd always care and wouldn't leave. But, I always said that one day when he needs me the most, I'll finally have the courage to turn my back and just walk away. It turned out I didn't have to; he did it for me.

I miss everything we had together, but I guess nothing lasts forever. He's still in my heart, though. It might take a while to forget everything because to me, everything had a special meaning. When I lost him, I felt like I lost a part of myself that I'd never get back.

Whoever said it's better to have loved and lost than never to have loved at all obviously didn't lose much love in their lives. I wish I had never fallen so deeply in love. That way, I wouldn't know what I was missing. I wouldn't know what all the fuss was about or how amazing it can feel in someone else's arms. I didn't just lose him, I lost myself and I lost my future, the one I thought of with him in it. I lost my faith; the faith that someone truly can love me and not leave me. I lost my trust in love.

But that is the story of my life and I have to find ways to cope with this loss. I have to find strength where none previously existed. I have to find the future that depends solely on me. I have to find hope at the end of this long, dark tunnel. I have to find faith that there are people who love me enough to see my worth. I have to somehow regain my trust in people. And perhaps what will be the hardest thing for me is realizing I have to learn to let go of the idea that he was my be all and end all. There is someone else out there for me. I just have to be ready to let them in. So, I guess I need to start with Mikeo and let him in. Who knows? He may be the one that my heart will love again.

Chapter 15

The Day After

Thank God it's Friday. It's been a long week, and I'm going to take the day off to clean my house and relax. I had a great time with Mikeo. I slept on it last night and decided to give him a chance to win my heart. I will try this love thing again. Maybe it'll work out for me this time. Speaking of which, I'm going to call him. I wonder if he's up, Kay contemplated

"Good morning, handsome. Rise and shine. Are you up?"

"Yes, my queen."

"Thank you for the lovely night. I had an amazing time."

"It was my pleasure. You seem to be a new person today," Mikeo commented.

"Yes. I did some thinking, and I've decided to give you a chance and stop fighting my feelings for you. I actually feel the same way you do and that scares me because we really haven't known each other that long."

"You can't stop what's meant to be, and that's us being together," Mikeo stated. "I have to go off and take care of some business, but I will talk to you later."

After hanging up, Kay stood there staring at the phone, going over the thoughts in her head.

What should I do first? Hmmm, I haven't talked to the girls since we had drinks at the Blue Martini Lounge. We need to talk and set things straight. I have to put my foot down. I won't stand for them treating me like a little puppy anymore. They better get used to the new Kay.

Kay went on about her business cleaning up and then relaxing while thinking back on the night she spent with Mikeo. She still couldn't believe how quickly her feelings for him had grown. When she looked out the window, she saw that the flowers that covered the walkway hours ago were cleaned up. She smiled at the memory of them laid out on the ground.

As soon as she walked into the kitchen, the doorbell rang. Speaking of the devils, it was Val and Shawn. Kay opened the door and her whole mood changed. She knew the time had come for her to set the record straight with them once and for all.

Chapter 16

Putting My Foot Down

"Hello, ladies. Come in. I was just thinking of you and was going to call you later to talk."

"Yeah, we need to talk to you as well," Val commented. "See, you been acting funny since you call yourself having a man now. You must have lost your mind. Did you forget that you are nobody without us?"

Shawn added to Val's insults. "See, when you big girls get a man or think you have a man, you start thinking you have it made. No, it doesn't work like that. Men who start dating people like you are not serious about you. They won't take you home to their mom and introduce you to their friends. They want someone they can look good with. Only thing they want you fat women for is cooking, cleaning, and keeping them warm in the cold that's it."

Kay stood there with her fists balled up wanting to beat them both down until no one knew who they were. Instead, she decided to be the bigger person. She was shocked that the two people who she trusted and considered friends switched on her all because of a man. Kay couldn't believe what she was hearing and realized at that instant they were both jealous of her. They used to be her girls. Now they'd quickly become enemies.

How can they let a man come between us? True friends don't allow this. This so-called friendship is officially over as of this moment, Kay thought

"Let me tell you two scheming, conniving heifers something. How dare you come in my house and insult me this way! As of this moment, we're not friends any longer. I will not allow you to talk to me and look down on me like that anymore. I've been the holding you two down ever since we were kids. I'm the one who helped you both get to where you are now. The mere fact that you two can come at me like this so easily shows me what you're really all about, you used me, but that's cool. Just remember you were the ones who needed me. I didn't need you. One thing's for certain though, you'd best believe you won't be using me anymore! I don't need friends that smile in my face and stab me in the back. What's wrong with me being big and having a man? I tell you what; you both need to get out of my house before there's a serious misunderstanding in here!"

Shawn and Val had surprised looks on their faces. I bet neither one of them thought I would ever build up the nerve to stand up to them. All I could do then was stand strong and pray that God gave me strength and guidance to free myself from those leeches.

Lord, speak to my heart and give me the continued courage to break away from this. Give me a message of love, not a message of hate. Help me to forgive them, because they don't know any better. Guide me. Give me your word; help me to promote a healing for their hatred. I don't know what to do. I need you to comfort me, guide me, strengthen me, and sustain me. Amen. Kay silently prayed.

I stood there holding my door open, waiting for them to make their exit. Shawn stepped in my face and said, "I don't care if we're friends or not. You always thought you were better than us. You never talked down on us and yes, you helped us, but we've always felt like you thought you owned us. You walk around like you can't be touched, and we're sick of your "holier than thou" attitude. That's why I'm gonna have to bring you down a notch. I'm about to school you. You want to know the real reason why Zylin broke up with you? It's because we started going out together. That's right; we were messing around behind your back. You were always bragging about how good he was to you and how great he was in bed, so I had to find out. I wanted to see for myself what it felt like to have a good man instead of the no-good dogs I kept getting. So I took what you had. Come to find out, it wasn't hard at all. Turned out he was a dog just like the others, always chasing after a bone. Once I got him and found out what he was really about, I didn't need him anymore. I just wanted to see what was so special about him."

Val stood on the threshold of my doorway cackling before she added, "Allow me to tell you a short but sweet story; I am sleeping with Mikeo. In fact, I sexed him up really good right before your date!"

Shawn laughed out loud and said, "Oh! You too? He's good in bed, isn't he!"

They stood there high-fiving each other and reveling in my anguish.

My heart dropped down to my stomach. I started feeling sick and getting hot like I was about to vomit. Before I knew it, I reached out and grabbed Shawn, pushing her past Val and out the door.

While they were stumbling to regain their footing, I yelled, "I feel sorry for the both of you because you will never know what it's like to be a real friend. You two need to get out of my face before I hurt you something serious. I never want to see either of you again. You're both dead to me."

Once they collected themselves, Val turned around and said, "You'll never have a man who loves and wants you the way you want them to. They don't want you. They just want your money, just like we did. Your fat behind think you're better than us, but guess what? You're not. You think Mikeo really likes you? You think he really cares about you? Before you get in the game to play with the big girls, you need to learn how to play the game. We win, you lose."

Chapter 17

The Pain

After Val and Shawn finally left, Kay fell down on her knees and started crying. The tears fell freely and she made no attempt to stop them. She asked herself how she could be so blind. Looking back, everything started to make sense. How Shawn and Zylin would always be too friendly with each other or how they would go out and say they were just hanging out having fun. She was her friend, so she didn't think anything of it. They were way too close when she came back home to visit on the holidays. Not knowing what else to do, she started to pray.

"Lord, I belong to you. Why did you allow this to happen to me? My life is not my own, I gave you everything. I lived the way you wanted me to live and this is what I get? How could you do this to your child? I feel abandoned and lost now. Always feeling like it was my fault, I blamed myself. I need your help, some understanding. Hear my cry, Lord. I'm crying out to you. Attend to me, take away my pain. Put your healing hands on me, Lord so I can be recovered. The wind is blowing hard within me and I can't breathe. Strengthen me, rescue me, and hold me. My heart is in my hands and I'm giving it to you to restore so I can go on. I'm on my knees begging you to remove any hate in me, Lord. I have to get up and take my place. I don't know how, but I know I'll make it. I made up my mind and I will keep going until I finish. I know you did this for a reason. Lord, all I need is a touch from you. Lord, I'm standing in the need of prayer. When I call, I know you're there. Just reach your hand out, touch me, and make it right. I know whatever I go through you will bring me through. Help me to remember that if I just hold on, it will come. In your name, I pray. Amen."

Chapter 18

Two Days Later

Diary,

It's been two days since I've talked to anyone. I haven't accepted Mikeo's phone calls or my job's. I've been lying in my bed crying and feeling sorry for myself. But, I know I have to talk to Mikeo about this soon. I have to hear his side of the story. I'm trying to forgive Shawn and Val. I know I need to, but I have to keep asking God to help me on it. I keep asking myself how could he ask to date me when he was sleeping with them. Did he plan this? Did he really mean everything he'd said? I don't know whether to believe or trust him anymore. I'm so messed up right now. I have to get myself together and talk to him. It's time to get to the bottom of this.

Ignoring the butterflies in her stomach, Kay reached for the phone and speed-dialed that familiar number. As soon as he answered, Kay spoke.

"Hello, Mikeo, I need to talk to you. Would you come over?"

"Yes, of course. What's wrong? I've been calling you and your voicemail kept picking up. Are you sick? Are you okay? I was worried about you."

"I don't feel like talking over the phone. What time will you be over?"

"In about ten minutes. Do you need me to bring you anything?"

"No, that's okay. I'll see you then."

She got up to freshen up and put on some clothes. While getting dressed, she said a quick and silent prayer. *Give me an open ear to hear what he has to say. Let me have an open heart. Give me a discerning spirit to know if he's telling me the truth and the strength to accept whatever he tells me.*

Chapter 19

The Truth

Kay was waiting patiently for Mikeo to arrive and so much was going through her head. It felt so good when he told her how he felt because she felt the same way. Now there is confusion, frustration, and hurt. Kay's thoughts were interrupted by a knock on the door and she knew it was Mikeo. She didn't give him any time to say anything when she opened the door. Kay waited for him to come in and she got straight to the point.

"Mikeo, I haven't been answering your calls because I was dealing with something that was brought to my attention concerning you. You know that Shawn, Val, and I were best friends, right? Well, the other day they told me that you're sleeping with both of them. I need to know is that true."

Mikeo's head dropped and then he looked at her. He sounded dejected as he began to speak.

"Kay, I'm sorry. I don't know what to say. I was sleeping with them when we first started out and then I cut it off with them. I told them that I didn't want to go on like that because I started to get feelings for you. At first, I was talking to you just to get a quick lay, but as I got to know you, it wasn't like that anymore. Everything I said to you that night was the truth. Please believe me."

Her eyes welled up with tears as she felt the remnants of a broken heart crumble and disintegrate. Sadly, she sat on the sofa and looked up at him.

Shaking her head, she said, "I can't believe this, Mikeo! Why didn't you just tell me? You let me fall in love with you knowing you were screwing my friends behind my back. How could you do that to me? You said you wanted a family with me. You wanted to share your life with me and you do this? Why would you break my heart? You of all people should know what it feels like to have someone play with your emotions and crush your heart to pieces. Just when it felt good to know that I can love again, you prove me wrong."

Knowing the seriousness of the situation, Mikeo looked deeply into her eyes and said, "Kay, to be honest with you, I don't have words to make you feel better or to even explain why I did it. The only thing I can do is to ask for your forgiveness. I don't blame you for being angry. My heart is aching to see you like this and knowing I'm the source that has caused you so much pain.

I don't want to lose you. It's hard enough thinking you may hate me right now, but I don't want to live my life feeling like I meant absolutely nothing to you. I was wrong; I thought I knew what I wanted when I first met you. I had no idea that what I wanted and what I needed were two entirely different things. I was afraid to be hurt again, so I made sure I never allowed another woman to get that close to me. But you...you changed me. You were able to break through that barrier in my heart and I started to look at you in a different light. I broke it off with them before we went out and I've laid my out true intentions for you. Give it a chance, Kay."

Kay looked at him with tears streaming down her face. "I don't know, Mikeo. I think if you had told me off the top that you were sleeping with them, I might could have dealt with it better. How am I supposed to trust that you've ended it with them? This is just too much for me to handle right now. I think it'd be best if you leave."

She walked over to the front door and opened it slowly. Mikeo stood in front of Kay and started to say something, but when he saw her refusal to acknowledge him, he exited the house with his shoulders slumped. As Kay shut the door, she noticed something very strange. For some reason, she felt as if a huge weight had been lifted off her shoulders. For the first time in her life, she realized she'd accepted herself and that she was no longer worried about what people thought of her. Shawn and Val would never be her friends again, but in all honesty, she owed them big time. Kay thanked them silently for what they'd done for her because they were the ones who showed her that she was not the person she used to be.

Chapter 20

Fragile Heart

I can't give up. I have to keep trying and give him a chance. Everybody makes mistakes. Lord, I am giving you back my fragile heart. You are the only one who can fix it. I hate crying night and day. I need you to embrace and love me, Lord. I know I can let it go.

Can I give him another chance? Can I completely open my heart again and risk him breaking it? He made me feel safe and loved. I've opened up my heart once before and got burned. He gave me hope; Mikeo showed me that love doesn't have to hurt. My heart is like a flower that needs water to blossom and grow. Everything I thought I couldn't have, he showed me I could.

Don't I deserve someone? Don't I deserve to be happy? I'm tired of being alone. Lord, did I make the right choice? Am I blinded by me being lonely?

Chapter 21

The End

Mikeo

It's been two weeks and Kay hasn't spoken to me. She's been very distant. She has every right to be angry with me. I know I was wrong. I don't want to lose her, but I think I already have. There has to be a way I can show her that I really do love her and want to have a family with her. I'm going to try and reach out to her to see if she'll meet me. Maybe if she sees me, it'll be easier for me to convince her to forgive me.

Kay

Two whole weeks has gone by since that whole debacle and I'm slowly coming around to being normal again, whatever that may be. I haven't talked to Shawn or Val since they told me how they really felt about me. It's funny, I don't even miss them. What's even better is that I don't feel I need their approval anymore.

***

The buzzing sound of a text message coming from the phone invaded Kay's thoughts. Looking at the screen, she was surprised to see it was from Mikeo. The message read: *Hello, beautiful. Please meet me on Flagler Drive by the university at seven o'clock p.m. wear something nice, I have a surprise for you.*

The first thought that popped into her head was to ignore the text. Her second mind tried to coerce her to text him and tell him that she wasn't interested. Kay's heart, on the other hand, wasn't having any of that. Her fingers danced over the screen and ending up sending one simple word: *Okay.*

Suddenly, her brain kicked into overdrive as Kay looked at the time. It's five o'clock already, and it takes about an hour to get there. *I'll just have to shower, throw something on right quick, and put my hair up. I better make sure to grab a sweater. It'll be cool out there,* she thought.

When she arrived at the destination, she faintly heard some music playing. As Kay stepped out of the car, a young man took her hand and guided her over to where Mikeo was waiting. He had a beautiful blanket laid out with some white wine and in the background "Slow Jam" by Monica and Usher was playing. He took her hand and asked if he could have this dance.

It was beautiful out, the sun was setting, giving the sky lots of glorious colors, and the cool breeze felt nice. Kay started to feel bad because she didn't take her time to get ready.

As the song ended, Mikeo got down on his knees and said, "I hold out my hands to you. One hand slowly unfolds, revealing to you the key to my heart. My other hand holds the password to my soul. These two gifts I place in your hand along with the third gift, the one that bounds the other two together. This gift is my love. These three gifts I give to you freely, my heart, my soul, and my love. As I place my hand over top of yours, I want you to know that they are yours to keep forever. Now you hold all that I am and all that I have in your hands. I want you to know, I love you and from the bottom of my heart, I'm asking you... will you marry me?"

Kay's heart started skipping a staccato beat. Her mouth went completely dry and she didn't know what to say. She was in shock. Everything seemed to be going in slow motion. As she stood there crying, the only thought running through her mind at that point was how much she loved this man. The next thing she knew, he was putting the ring on her finger while she was saying yes.

A year passed and their special day had finally arrived. They got married on the same beach they'd gone to on our first date. The two shared that day with close friends and family. Kay never talked to Shawn or Val again. It's a shame how their friendship ended, but life goes on. Their sidekick moved on and decided to live. If there was one thing she could say to them, she'd tell them that she forgave them and that three did play the game and she won.

Sometimes close friends are lost, but so much more is gained in the end. She will never belittle herself again and allow people to make her doubt herself. Big, Bold and Beautiful; that's who she is.

Big Bold Beautiful Woman

Flash Fiction

Why do you look at me with that undefined look of yours? Is it that you like what you see, or is it my curves that turn you on with poor desires of me? Is it my beauty, personality, my comfort spot? Maybe it's the walk that I walk with lighting electricity that turns you on. Or is it that you're scared of what people might say about you because you're with me?

You don't have to tell me. I know. I am beautiful yet dangerous. From the curves of my body, to the walk that I walk, to the smile I smile. You don't have to be afraid of this BIG, BOLD WOMAN. This woman will be the best you ever had. See, my personality oversees my looks, my beauty oversees my looks, and my walk tells the story of my life. They tell the tale that I am a STRONG, BIG, BOLD WOMAN that walks on fire with desires of achievements.

From the fashions I wear to the boldness and confidence I have. UNIQUE from all sides and corners, I came to terms with who I am a long time ago. I walk with my head held high; I shine like a star in the sky.

Are you afraid to release yourself to see the beauty that stands in front of you? I am a BIG, BOLD WOMAN with full lips, hips, eyes, and thighs. If you look deeper, you will find what lies and realize that the complexity of my diversity does not define me. It moves me, inspires me, and uplifts me.

My flaws encourage me to love myself and always do my best. They set me apart from the rest. I am unique. I am different. I am who God wants me to be. Big waist, big frame, and thick in the thighs...this is who I am. No deceit, no lies, curly locs, brown eyes, a smile that will light up the skies, and a caramel tone that will sweeten up your day. Rich inside because that's what my God says I am. Polished like a diamond, I embrace who I am. Confident, not conceited, just love who I am with no doubts. My character speaks for itself. Now are you going to love and accept me like I should be? I don't need you to validate me.

Now I know what it takes. You can't hurt me, use me, mistreat me, or abuse me. It's no longer a delusion. I have the power to love me and I'm God's creation. Yes, a Master plan even in the absence of a man. I will still stand tall, refusing to fall. See, my confidence and self-esteem exudes all over. I refuse to let anyone take that away from me. I am bold, triumphant, and radiant. I have insecurities; however, this is the body God gave me.

Embracing me is the most liberating thing I have ever done. I no longer stare in the mirror and try to find myself. Instead, I point out the most beautiful things about myself. I've always looked to the mirror to tell me what I really looked like. I let the reflection of me be the definition of me. Never mind who I really was, the mirror had all the answers. But, what it didn't show was the most important characteristics that needed to be seen, the inner reflections of the golden, warm-hearted, generous, and loving person I am. So I no longer go to the mirror to be defined.

Growing up as the fat girl who was pretty but not good enough to date is a tough cross for any girl to bear. I will redefine BIG, BOLD, BEAUTIFUL WOMEN in my own way. I took all the negatives turned them to positives and loosened those barriers for me to be free. I will no longer dream to be someone I have already become. The scar that I bear from life is an honor and I will bare all marks and be proud of them.

BIG, BOLD WOMAN...we are unique, talented, successors, nurturing, sexy, alluring, and sensual; a fighter equipped for anything. We come in all shapes and sizes—thick and voluptuous; plenty to love. We are courageous and fearless entrepreneurs, CEO's, presidents, and executives. Our history, legacy, and journey incorporate in our life quest. Unstoppable, a voice that is heard everywhere; we sing our own melody, walking within our own density.

Ladies, walk with fire under your feet. It is the strength and glow that shines from within. It is the essence of who we are, not wavering to become something we are not. It's the drive that keeps us going, the lessons that keep us knowing and the harvest that we reap from the seeds of deeds that we keep sowing resulting in blossoming gifts that keep growing. Don't let anything defeat you no matter what it is.

BIG, BOLD WOMAN...let's inspire people to let go of the hang-ups of trying to achieve some phony, externally imposed ideal of physical perfection. When we accept ourselves and invite our people to accept themselves, we become Bold, Unforgettable, Breathtaking, Symbolic, Powerful, and Undefeated.

This is us...BIG and BOLD.   BIG, BOLD WOMAN...a big heart and a bold spirit.

She is fearfully and wonderfully made

Handcrafted by the Master and Creator of all things

She is worth far more than rubies, diamonds, and pearls

She wears her beauty better than any cover girl

She walks with her head held high and a swing in her hips

She is confident of her authenticity

She is witty and wise beyond her years

She works through her pain with silent tears

She weathers every storm with strength and tenacity

She is a woman of action, a mover, and a shaker

She welcomes every challenge

She's a risk-taker

There are no weaknesses to stand in her way

When she speaks, every mountain begins to sway

She is your mother, your sister, and friend

She lives within you so that you can ascend

A big heart and a bold spirit

This woman is you!

Poem Written By Michelle Starling Clark

Thank you, Michelle, my beautiful cousin and sister, for writing this poem. It goes right with what I am relating to in Big, Bold, and Beautiful Woman.